To Roger,
Best wishes
Denis

SEPT '11

CUBA

DENIS PRICE

authorHOUSE®

AuthorHouse™ UK Ltd.
500 Avebury Boulevard
Central Milton Keynes, MK9 2BE
www.authorhouse.co.uk
Phone: 08001974150

First published by AuthorHouse 9/7/2010

ISBN: 978-1-4520-6217-4 (sc)

This book is printed on acid-free paper.

To Rita...for everything

CHAPTER ONE

There was no sound, they were mainly children with faces twice their normal size and with bodies scorched black. Those with discernable mouths were screaming, silently of course, and holding up hands with fingers welded together. An adult sat alone and trembling with skin collected around his waist like a half removed shirt. Aid workers moved impotently among the victims with nothing but cigarettes and prayers to offer.

'Lights!' Shouted the Instructor, and the film's depiction of horror temporarily flickered away as the end of the projector`s hum coincided with the eye rubbing glare of reality. `Thank fuck for that,' he thought as he fumbled for his cigarettes. 'Couldn`t take much more of it, I'm sure that bastard enjoys showing us all this crap'. He drew in deeply on his cigarette and began instantly to cough. 'Are you alright mate?' said a voice from the next seat as he tried to smother his cough. 'Yeah, I`ll be okay thanks, it`s these cheap fags, they'll be the death of me'. He laughed weakly. 'Here, have one yourself'. His offer was declined as the Instructor announced re-commencement in five minutes.

He was in the Camp Cinema, used mainly for instructional purposes its original role had been to brief and de-brief wartime bomber crews. He looked around, smoke swirled around thickly and spiralled upward to the curved Nissen shaped roof. Its few windows were firmly shut resisting the fresh air and light of the autumnal world outside. I`m in the cheap seats again he thought as the usual seating arrangements decreed that officers sat at the front with subordinates behind.

The Instructor's cry of 'Lights!' plunged the hut into immediate darkness and ended the subdued muttering. The harsh probing beam of the projector, wreathed in smoke and accompanied by a muted hum continued to reveal man`s inhumanity to man as the film progressed in its stark black and white. Aid workers were shown with a group of soldiers, some sitting and some lying on improvised beds. The intrusive camera closed in on the suffering men dribbling and vomiting from swollen noses and mouths and excreting faeces and blood. Their pillows were dark with falling hair as they reached out to the probing camera with imploring swollen eyes.

The silence of the film equalled the silence in the cinema. He felt a need to cough and put up a hand to stifle the sound. Not because it would break the silence but more because of the moment. It would be like taking the piss, providing a cynical soundtrack to the suffering depicted on the screen. Ever the voyeur the camera panned sideways to another group again lying and sitting. Aid workers gently placed cigarettes between distended burnt lips, holding them to be smoked by men who's skin hung down like rags. The film continued in its silent chronicle of suffering showing tiny burnt bodies in defiant pugilistic poses having lost their fight against the fiery phosphorous.

He closed his eyes to it all attempting to shut it out. Think good things, he must think good things. He knew what it was all about, knew what they were doing, well practised at it they were. 'Sicken 'em, better still, frighten the shit out of 'em, get 'em to hate and even if we can't get 'em to do that, as long as they do as they're told we've achieved something.'

With eyes firmly closed and arms tightly folded, the insistent probing beam of the projector still sought him out. For Christ's sake he thought, don't let 'em win. Think good things, a pair of thrusting tits in a tight blouse, the gentle smooth curve of a waist as it swells out into full rounded buttocks, the girl in the shop yesterday. He wouldn't mind unzipping her overall, anything but endure this shit. He briefly opened his eyes to glance at the screen. A scorched swollen figure was vomiting a dark liquid into a bowl. He closed them again. Mustn't let the bastards win, they're clever they know what they're doing. They've silenced us all, forty grown men, nobody coughs, nobody belches and nobody farts, now that is an achievement. C'mon, more good things think more good things, the bird in the shop, and me going to Uni if this lot'll let me out in time, and Ernie, good old Ernie. C'mon Ern you've got to get better. The film flickered on and as he'd hoped his mind wandered. He'd been with Ernie at Maralinga, South Australia where the 'A' Bombs were tested, he was Codes and Ciphers and Ern was an Aircraft Engineer. They'd had some great times out there, he smiled to himself. Ernie was a crack shot, what about that time they went dingo hunting! Ernie had shot this bloody great dingo from the Landrover at close range and then climbed out with a bush knife to collect its tail, payment was per tail. He'd just reached it when the fucking great thing stood up on all fours utterly outraged, and went for him. He could still see him leaping aboard and screaming with this fucking great monster inches from his arse. He couldn't stop laughing for weeks. Yeah, he's a good lad Ern.

'Lights!' The silence was broken and horror flickered away at the Instructor's command. The probing beam faded together with the constant hum of the projector. It was back to eye-rubbing reality. 'Gentlemen, there'll be a ten minute break,' said the Instructor. The 'Gentleman' bit was in deference to the group of officers occupying the front row of seats.

'Thank God for that,' said a voice next to him. He turned and answered, 'Yeah, couldn't take much more of it meself, I'm sure that bastard enjoys it all.' He fumbled for his cigarettes, lit up and drew in deeply. 'Oh sorry mate.' He offered a cigarette, 'Smoke?' 'No ta, trying to give it up, you're new here aren't you?' The accent was thick Scouse. 'Yeah, only arrived yesterday, still settling in, didn't expect to cop for all this 'Protect and Survive' shite, done it all before anyway.'

'I'm George,' said the Scouser.

He reached across and shook hands, 'Dan', he said.

'It's all this Cuba crap,' said George.

'Whaddya mean?'

'You know, have the Russkies got missiles on Cuba or not?'

'Oh yeah, me mind's full of toasted Japs,' he said with a callous bravado he didn't feel. He inhaled deeply and began to cough and splutter. 'Are you okay?' said the Scouser, concerned as the coughing continued. 'Yeah I'll be alright thanks.' He smiled weakly, sure you won't have one?'

The Scouser shook his head and smugly popped a mint into his mouth as he began to read his 'Survivor's Notes.' Fair enough he thought, mebbe I should cut down a bit.

Bored, he began to take in his surroundings. The Cinema's war-time use was reflected in the signs in faded paint on the walls. Directions to air –raid shelters, black-out instructions, exhortations to 'Be like Dad and keep Mum!'. The building's few windows were firmly shut trapping its occupants in a thick soup of stale smoke and body odour. Christ, he thought, a room for mushroom men, kept in the dark and fed on crap. Just how much has this room seen? How many smooth faced twenty year olds sat on these seats thickening the air with their cigarettes and nervous farts as their nightly target was revealed? Thank Christ he wasn`t sat in this room seventeen years ago. His target was to get out of this lot and into real life, he'd done his bit but would the powers that be see it that way? This Cold War Cuba stuff didn't help. He could almost hear them reciting the obstacles. ' Forget it, we've educated you and trained you at the tax payer's expense and now when you're needed you expect to be released at a time when reservists are being called up and all discharges put on hold.'

He continued his survey of the room. From the concrete floor to the domed roof the paint was the standard Air Ministry cream. Metal and canvas chairs stood in serried ranks facing a small stage currently supporting a cinema screen. The projectionist was housed in his box at the rear of the room. Fire and sand buckets stood idle and full of used cigarette ends. Recognition charts showing Soviet aircraft were glued to the wall adding to the detritus of the previous war. What was next he wondered, more of the same? I've seen enough fucking horror films courtesy of Her Majesty to last a lifetime, what with 'The Horrors of VD' and 'The Liberation of Belsen' and now this obscenity.

The brisk rapping of the Instructor's pointer halted the dull murmur of voices and with a theatrical leap onto the stage, only pausing to genuflect to the officers, he announced that the training would continue with a guest speaker. The Scouser nudged him and whispered.

'What do you think to him then?'

'He's a flash bastard, young for a warrant officer, trying to impress is he?'

'Dead right, he's after a commission, makes no bones about it.'

'Right, he certainly looks the part anyway.'

'Yeah, you married?'

'No , why?'

'Just wondered if you needed a warning, he can't keep it in his pants, supposed to be shagging a bloke's wife over at Kenningly right now.'

'Dangerous for him innit?'

'You'd think so but he gets away with it.'

The guest speaker was being announced as Doctor Somebody or Other from the Atomic Research Establishment at Aldermaston. He groaned inwardly, spare us yet another ball achingly boring superbrain. Jesus he'd seen 'em before, all Physics and no personality. This one came as a shock. With eyes gleaming the Instructor solicitously helped a petite, attractive blonde woman in her mid thirties, dressed in a smart business suit on to the stage. A buzz of interest rose from the all male audience as she introduced herself. Speaking with a slight foreign intonation she elaborated on her background.

'Bit of alright this one.' said the Scouser.

'Yeah, makes a change.'

'Hey just look at him, he's got a hard on already, told you didn't I?'

'Okay, let's hear her then.'

Her field was nuclear physics she said but political science was another area of her interests. To begin with she would have to re-visit the film.

'Oh fucking hell!'

The lights went out and so did the audience's view of the speaker. He closed his eyes as the seductive voice described in detail the disintegration of the human body when subjected to nuclear inspired blast, fire and radiation. It seemed that the Hiroshima victims in the silent film with their death agonies being played out behind her were the unlucky ones. She was dead right there! You didn't have to go to college to learn that. No, the really lucky ones were instantly vaporized, situated as they were in the epicentre of the explosion. The Hiroshima bomb, the mere equivalent of thirteen kilotons of TNT, had detonated at two thousand feet over the city instantly killing between seventy and a hundred thousand 'lucky ones.' The 'unlucky ones' being shown dying on the screen had limbs blown off by blast borne debris and skin stripped from their bodies by heat blast. Those furthest away from the epicentre would suffer radiation sickness where the internal molecular structure of living cells would break down and internal organs turn to mush. This would be evidenced by unquenchable thirst, vomiting, hair loss and the gradual peeling away of skin. The seductive foreign intonation in the speaker's voice was becoming more evident as with practiced ease she recited the nuclear way of death.

His eyes were closed but his ears were open. He felt an irritation in his chest. What the hell was she on about now? Haven't we heard enough of this shit? I'm gonna be one of the unlucky ones anyway if I'm down in the bunker. Best to try and stay on top and get vaporized, won't feel a thing then. Kenningly's just up the road, the Red Menace'll have us bang to rights at the top of their target list, yeah, being vaporized sounded good he thought.

The irritation in his chest was getting worse, Jesus he couldn't cough now not with that crap on the screen. Hand tight over his mouth he opened his eyes, the film had moved on. Thank God no more burnt kids, we're on to mushroom clouds now. She was well in her stride, her silhouetted figure was moving coquettishly in front of the screen where behind her somebody's peaceful Pacific Island paradise was being engulfed by a mushroom cloud.

His chest was heaving, he couldn't contain himself any longer and fell into a paroxysm of coughing and retching. The speaker paused, she couldn't see him through the gloom, he spluttered his 'sorries' between gasps. George the Scouser slapped him on the back.

'Are you alright mate?'

'Yeah yeah I'll be okay.'

An authoritative voice from the front asked if he needed fresh air? No, he'd be alright thanks. The woman's voice asked if he was well and would he like a drink of water? He thanked her and said no. The disturbance over, chairs scraped and the speaker continued.

George had given him a mint. He'd rather have a fag but the mint helped ease his chest. She was now describing a one megaton bomb's capacity for destruction. How it was estimated that the Soviet's first salvo on the United Kingdom would be comprised of about eighty of 'em which would equal three point five tons of high explosive for every inhabitant. Initial casualties would be in the region of between two point five and nine million. Difficult to be accurate of course but an attack of that capacity would reduce the United Kingdom to a wasteland.

All he wanted to do was laugh. It was surreal. In the middle of all this apocalyptic fucking horror this nice attractive woman with the lexicon of terror at her fingertips had solicitously asked a bloke with a cough if he'd like a drink of water. It's a madhouse, a fucking madhouse. The film behind her flickered and clicked to a halt. She was in discussion with the Instructor, it was slides now and she'd gone political. 'You may smoke gentlemen', she said, choosing to ignore that almost all were anyway. With the lights momentarily back on he knew that in the role of serial cougher he would be a target . Several turned heads from the front row confirmed his suspicions. They'd be wondering, was he genuine or was he taking the piss? Having only arrived the previous day he was an unknown, a suspect. He could almost hear 'em.

'Who is that man? Get me his name.'

Later, in the Officer's Mess bar over gins and tonics he could imagine the conversation.

'There we were in the middle of this scientist totty's bit on mutually assured destruction when some oik at the back decides to choke to death. Almost made a good job of it as well.'

'Was he genuine? Another voice would say. 'Or was he just being bloody subversive, you know what some of them are like, attention span of a gnat!'

The room was dark again. A slide was being shown of a map of Europe extending eastward to Turkey and the southern Soviet Union. Using the Instructor's pointer the female visitor was indicating missile sites and airbases both NATO and Warsaw Pact and speculating on the latter's nuclear capability. His speculation was of a different order as he studied her every movement and gesture. What is it about women? She knows how she's being looked at. There's forty of us here all watching her, lusting after her wanting to explore the secrets of breast and thigh. He wondered, she has power and authority and knows we have to listen and be attentive, to nod to smile and even applaud if necessary. She knows all this, we're all her captives but not of her Government appointed status, we're all subservient to her sexuality. She's watching us watch her and she's prepared herself for it. Her style of dress, her voice and gestures, all served up to deliver to a male audience.

He shifted around in the uncomfortable seat, Christ!

How much longer? The seat wasn't the real problem, it was the sexual arousal that even the thick blue serge couldn't disguise. Go on love get on with it, you tell us how to destroy the world and then we'll get together for a good shag! The slide changed to a close-up of American missile sites based in Turkey, all threatening the Soviet Union. With the pointer indicating upward at the slide the soft foreign inflected voice wrapped itself languorously around place names such as Izmir, Anatolia, Erzerum and Adapazari. He glanced to the left and right of his row of seats, even in the gloom he could see they were entranced. This was real power, telling her audience who she was and what was expected of them.

The slide projector clicked and stopped. 'Well gentlemen' she said and smiled winningly. 'That concludes my part in the presentation, are there any questions?' The pointer was now directed downward as she glanced enquiringly at the front row. The Instructor, who'd sat himself with the officers immediately raised his arm. George nudged him, 'See, told you didn't I, creeping bastard."

His question was the obvious one. 'What was the likelihood of Soviet missiles being based on Cuba and what would be the reaction of the United States if this took place?'

She paused and after clearing her throat, answered by saying that as always, diplomatic efforts had to be made to resolve the crisis. Military confrontation was the last resort. She went further by saying that many believed that the whole crisis was only Premier Khruschev's testing of the resolve of the new young President Kennedy although this was an interpretation she did not share. What was certain was that under no circumstances would the Americans allow Soviet missiles to be pointed at them in their own back yard. We live in troubled times she said, what with serious confrontation in Berlin and Korea we in the Free world must be prepared for any eventuality.

Well, he thought, that was a stirring reply. The Reader's Digest couldn't have put it better. She quickly asked if there were any more questions in a tone that suggested she didn't want any. A wag safely hidden away in the anonymity of the rear seats shouted, 'What are you doing tonight?' This was the stuff to give the troops. A guffaw of laughter swept through the room. She smiled coyly, thanked the enquirer telling him she had to be at home to prepare dinner for a husband and two kids but thanked him for the invitation anyway. The routine was then that she'd be swept away to the Officer's Mess Bar where this time there'd be no discussion over the identity of her hopeful admirer. Boys will be boys after all and it was good for morale, it was that bloody subversive interrupting her presentation who'd been the problem.

He watched as the senior of the officers smugly escorted her from the room leaving everyone else to the final aspect of the training, civil defence against nuclear attack. The Instructor, in his element, was back on stage clutching the pointer with an aide standing by to operate the slide projector. It was his chance to shine. George nudged him.' Here, you'd better have a couple of these.' He proffered his packet of mints. 'If you break up his presentation you'll be in deep shit.'

Thanking George he took them and began to stare at the lean athletic figure on the stage. He felt uneasy, there was something about the bloke that unsettled him. Had he met him before? He looked uncomfortably familiar. The strutting figure was being masterful with his aide who was fumblingly replacing the projector bulb. Sucking on a mint he weighed him up. Early to mid-thirties, about five feet eleven, average build, dark thick hair on top of a broad face. Then it hit him, of course, Christ, why hadn't he seen it sooner? He turned to George and whispered. 'I've just noticed something."

'What's that then?'

'He could be my brother."

The scouser paused. 'Yeah, I noticed that as soon as the lights came on, it's not a strong likeness though. With a bit of luck you'll look different in daylight.'

'I hope so, I'm twenty-five. He must have ten years on me'.

The pointer rapped firmly on the wooden stage. 'Your attention please gentlemen!'

The Instructor began, this was the final part of the proceedings, how to protect yourself against nuclear blast, fire and radiation. Sucking hard on his mint he closed his eyes. Of all the bullshit of the day this was the most unacceptable. Here we all are at the sharp end. We know exactly what'll happen to us and yet we're exhorted to fill sandbags, take off front doors and pile 'em up next to cupboards full of soil. He recalled the final insult which he'd first heard when doing basic training. It seemed that even a sheet of brown paper between the human body and the fire blast from a one megaton bundle of instant sunshine would offer some protection. In those early days his class had been bollocked rigid when they'd given a rousing collective cheer at this surreal bit of news. This Instructor ignored the brown paper advice which seemed a pity as there'd be a lot of it about to use.

He smiled grimly at his own joke.

The flash bastard was now talking over the slide with the dark silhouette of his pointer stabbing at the screen for emphasis.

'Of course, this is about civil defence,' he paused for effect, ' for civilians.' Somehow he made the word 'civilians' sound distasteful. Like a lot of career military personnel he regarded civilians as a lesser breed, 'untermenschen', feckless bastards who were inclined to get in the way. They'd get their four minute warning of course, survival depended on the four minute warning he said. The warning would come from Bomber Command Headquarters at High Wycombe. Passed to major Police Stations it would be activated by seven thousand power operated sirens all over the United Kingdom and be backed up by eleven thousand manual sirens located in village pubs, shops, hospitals and Coastguard Stations.

The slide changed behind the speaker. Cue earnest, portly, middle-aged figures in tin hats frozen on screen racing like the 'scramble' of long gone Battle of Britain pilots. Not toward revving Spitfires but to steel drums with winding handles like granny's old wringer.

George nudged him. 'Where the fuck are we when all this is going on?'

'Shush!'

A series of slides showed families stacking tins of food and water containers in their protected 'fallout room'. Superimposed across the final slide was the message '14

Days.' He thought of the images on the Hiroshima film, they were survivors of a sort. Would these people want their fourteen days if they knew what it was like to survive like those in the film? He thought not.

George's whispered question to him was now being answered. Yes, where the hell would we be when all this was going on? The flash bastard was holding forth. It seemed that in the event of hostilities which might possibly be on a tit for tat basis to begin with, for example they destroy Birmingham so we obliterate Leningrad. They destroy our Naval complex on the Solent so we destroy theirs at Murmansk. 'The tit for tat scenario is felt by those that know about these things to have some credence for after all, who wants to inherit a wasteland?' said the Instructor. 'Anyway, after the first strike the politicians will emerge to argue over what's left. The military gets time to re-form, lick its wounds so that's why we'll all be in the bunker.' There you are George he thought, there's your answer. Snug and cosy, elbow to elbow with our betters and all sharing the same tin of beans and pissing in the same pot, fucking wonderful and I'll bet they feel the same.

The slide show ended and the lights were on as the Instructor stood deferentially aside for the most senior officer to mount the stage. Tall, be-medalled and with a slight paunch he held up his hand needlessly to end the chatter. 'Yes, we were a team,' he said. First I'd heard of it he thought. His lot tell us what to do and we do it, or else! That was the usual drill. Funny that now we're all in the shit we're suddenly a team. The officer went on to say that they, that was him and his mates, were the planners, shorthand for brains of course, and we were the supporting specialists they couldn't do without. This was why there was a place for us thirty feet below ground directly beneath the operations room. In line with civil defence procedures all over the United Kingdom we would have food and water for three months although some would emerge before then in the appropriate protective clothing. Their task would be to check radiation levels. He wondered as he listened, would they call for volunteers from the newly designated team?

The officer paused and George raised his arm. 'A question sir.'

'Yes.'

He knew then that George was worried and taking it all seriously.

'If the worst comes to the worst will the Russians only attack military targets? What I mean is, we expect to be hit but what about our families in towns and cities, what about them?'

The officer cleared his throat noisily. 'Er yes, your concern is understood and shared by us all but I must impress on you that we are not yet at that stage. Needless to say President Kennedy and his advisers are discussing the Cuban situation with the Soviet Government as we speak. As America's closest NATO ally we are being kept fully informed of developments. What we do and say today is merely prudent preparation. Have no fear, you will all be put in the picture.' The officer looked toward the Instructor who sensing the finality of the answer called the room to attention allowing the group of officers to leave before the disarray of muttering figures jostled and jammed the narrow exit.

CHAPTER TWO

His cigarette smoke drifted lazily upward as he gently exhaled. Lying on his bed he watched as it gathered in the corner of the room above him. He'd noticed the threads of the web when he'd arrived yesterday. The dried out husks of two flies were telling the world the web was fully booked and occupied. He blew more smoke upward watching it as it drifted into the corner hanging like low cloud below the trapped husks. A sudden movement pleased him. Irritated by the smoke, the web's occupant had unravelled itself from its hidden corner and scuttling down a silver thread it disappeared downward out of view.

Lucky bastard that spider, he thought. He'd signed for the room yesterday, signed that it was clean and in good order. Ticked the itinerary, two beds, two tin lockers, two lamps, two chairs, two of everything, like Noah had just moved in. He hadn't ticked for a fucking spider though.

It was the standard two man room and he was lucky to be the only occupant, well him and the spider anyway, but it could stay. He liked spiders, they were like ants, industrious and tenacious, he admired that like he admired the female scientist at the lecture. That's what she wanted of course, admiration. It empowered her, the knowledge that she was physically admired added to the power her government granted status accorded her.

He glanced upward at the dried out husks fast in the web and smiled. There'd been forty of 'em caught in her web this afternoon.

Lying there his mind drifted back to his arrival. 'Granby!' The friendly bus driver had shouted. 'It's all yours mate, RAF Camp's across road.' Sweating on the unseasonally warm October morning he'd thanked the driver and dumped his holdall on the pavement. He felt vulnerable. The warm companionship of the bus was pulling away to God knows where leaving him with a twinge of apprehension at what lay ahead. Was Granby to be his last posting? Would they grant him an early release to take up his University place or would it be a cold rejection? Exigencies of the Service was the usual catch all. They'd be right of course, they wanted their money's worth, but bollocks, they'd had more than enough from him, he'd served seven years in every shithole they'd sent him to without demur, so a few months shouldn't make any difference.

He'd stood on the pavement watching as the companionship of the bus drew away and he was left to survey the main street. Until recently it had been part of the A1 trunk road, a conduit to people's lives teeming and bustling with traffic. Now by- passed, the detritus of its former vitality stood desolate and shabby. Cafes, garages, shops, unwanted and for sale, it was Klondyke when the gold had gone and the rush was over. All the street lacked was wind borne tumbleweed and a Frankie Lane voice- over.

'Are you looking for the RAF Camp?'

He'd turned to the female voice, it had broken his reverie. His practised eye quickly took in her appearance. Short, dark with pert good looks and a shapely figure her sober shop coat couldn't disguise.

'Er, Yeah.'

The girl nodded and looked at him quizzically. 'You're new aren't you?'

'Ellie, customer waiting!'

Before he could answer the shrill voice from inside the adjacent greengrocer's interrupted. Wordlessly the girl turned away to disappear into the darkness of the shop. Ellie, he thought as he stared after her, that's worth remembering. Picking up his holdall he'd trudged across the road following the friendly bus driver's instructions. RAF Granby occupied Granby Hall, an imposing Victorian residence commandeered by the military in the war and retained still as a Bomber Command Group Headquarters. Deceivingly tucked away only a few yards from the main thoroughfare, its main military entrance was decorated with the bold exhortation to 'Strike Hard, Strike Sure.'

Yeah, all that was yesterday he thought, and now I`m lying on my bed talking to a fucking spider. A movement caught his eye, the spider was creeping up the wall in short sharp bursts. He'd finished his smoke so it was going home, lucky bastard, he wished it was as simple for him. He watched as it passed the dried husks of the flies and scuttled to reach its web. The presence of the husks intrigued him. How could others be lured to a similar fate when former victims were left in full view? Jesus he thought, what's happening to me? I don't need this. He'd never liked occupying a room on his own. In theory it was wonderful, the privilege of rank, privacy, permission to personalise, all eagerly sought after. Trouble was he needed human contact, someone to moan to or at after coming off watch or returning pissed after a night out, otherwise you finish up like this, talking to a fucking spider.

Through the thin walls he could hear a radio beeping as precursor to the hourly news bulletin. It'd be good to hear the news after the events of the day, see how much longer we've got he thought drily. He felt in his holdall, still unpacked, and fished out a small pocket radio. Locating the news mid stream he heard the announcer confirm President Kennedy's intention of placing a naval blockade around Cuba, he called it a 'quarantine' to prevent the delivery of further Soviet missiles to the island.

So, that was why they'd had to listen to all that bullshit again! But how would the Russians react to all this? More to the point if it doesn't all blow over what were his chances of early release? But then it wouldn't matter anyway, nothing would, not any more.

There was a loud knock on his door and a voice asked to come in. Turning off the radio he shouted an affirmative knowing it was George whose room was further down the corridor.

'Too much of that and you'll go blind.' George said, grinning at him lying on his bed.

'I'm over here mate, over here.' He responded.

It was the stock response to an old joke. 'I've given up self abuse', he said, I talk to spiders instead, the intellectual challenge is more stimulating'.

'Don't worry, we've all got one, they're on the itinerary didn't you notice?' Said George.

He laughed and coughed pointing to a chair. The Scouser sat heavily asking him what he thought of the news on top of the day's training. George thought it was all a bit ominous. If it came to it he'd rather be back in Liverpool being vaporized with his nearest and dearest than stuck thirty feet underground farting beans for three months with a bunch of strangers. Lighting up he looked at George's disconsolate figure slumped in the chair. 'Don't worry about it' he told him, with a conviction he didn't feel, reminding him there'd been these Cold War scares before. 'Remember Berlin, with the tanks eyeball to eyeball at Checkpoint Charlie, all it needed was some gung-ho Lootenant to press a button and that would have been that! Common sense usually prevails, it has up to now'.

'That's an optimistic view, my trouble is I can understand how the Russians feel.' said George, 'Pissed off being surrounded by American missile sites, why shouldn't they put a few in Uncle Sam's backyard, see how the Yanks like that!'

'I know what you're saying,' he answered, 'But remember that bird poo-pooing the idea of Khruschev taking the piss out of Kennedy?'

'Yeah, so what?'

'Well I think there's something to it, just you watch, it'll all fizzle out when Mr. K's had his fun.'

George looked pensive and started to suck a mint. 'Christ I hope you're right, it's just that this time it seems more urgent, what with the lectures and that. Sometimes I wish we didn't know so much.' He had a point there. During the Hiroshima film he'd wanted to put his hand up, 'Please sir, can I be excused the horror, I've got a note from me mum.' The images remained, burnt, swollen irradiated bodies, still fresh as they were meant to be. What is the point of it all he thought? The average civvy hasn't a clue or a care. They listen and watch the same news that we do. Libraries are full of booklets on how to fill sandbags and hoard food and water, other than that life goes on. They get up in a morning, go to work, eat, sleep, shit, shave and shag, they haven't a care in the world.

George was staring at him intently. 'Are you worried at all, I mean really worried?'

He jumped up from his bed. 'C'mon, bugger this, all I'm worried about is what happens in Granby after seven o'clock?' Cheered up, George responded in the same tone. 'I thought you'd never ask. The choice is a limited one. It's either down to the TV room to watch 'University Challenge' or… He couldn't resist interrupting George, 'Over to you Jesus your starter for ten.' He mimicked the exaggerated public school drawl of the show's quizmaster, Bamber Gascoigne.

'Very good,' said George. 'As I was saying, or it's into Granby to sink twenty pints of sludge at the Green Dragon and then deflower half a dozen of the local virgins.'

'No contest.' he replied, 'the Green Dragon it is, I'll get me coat.' Autumn was making its presence felt as they walked along the tree lined avenue leading from their accommodation to the main gate. The light was fading like the colour of the falling leaves as they casually kicked at the shining horse chestnuts lying in their path.

'Was a time when I'd bust a gut for this lot, stick a six inch nail through 'em then soak 'em in vinegar. Like bloody cannonballs they were.' said George wistfully.

'You cheatin' scouse bastard, vinegar! Is nothing sacred?

'No, nothing you yorkie pillock,' said George with assumed vehemence. 'Nothing is sacred in the battle of the conkers.'

George picked up several. 'Here, keep these a few days, when they're hard we'll have a game.' He looked at the proffered horse chestnuts, damp and gleaming in their rich brown and cream tones.

'Go on.' said George, 'Take 'em.'

'Okay you soft sod, I can't believe I'm doing this, but no vinegar, that's cheating.'

George grinned and watched him put them in his pocket.

Security was as lax as ever as they walked through the main gate, acknowledging the nonchalant wave of the duty policeman. After a short walk along the lane they were back on the main street, the scene of his arrival the previous day. He glanced across the road at the greengrocer's where he'd met the girl. It was closed but he could see lights at the back of the building. They must live in he supposed and wondered if she was there? She might be if it's her family's shop, more likely she's hired help. Still, worth keeping an eye open. There was something about her.

He was dawdling and George was impatient. 'C'mon then, what's the hold up?'

'How long you been here George?'

'About four months.'

'Ever go in that greengrocer's shop?'

'No why?'

'Oh nothing."

George had warned him before they set off, it was Friday night, payday at the local pits. You'd to be careful Friday nights. It was well known that the men with the blue scarred knuckles and faces looked unkindly on liaisons with their women, real or imaginary. A good kickin' could often be the result. A high price to pay for a brief romantic interlude!

The Green Dragon was a rambling redbrick thirties pub which made no pretence of catering to the bourgeoisie, few Jaguars had ever been seen in its carpark. Strangers to Granby could be pardoned for confusing it with the sturdy public lavatory next door built in a similar utilitarian style. Like many pubs it was territorial. It had its 'snug,' the home of the ancients with their clacking dominoes and dentures. The grandly named 'Gainsborough Lounge' had its stab at sophistication ruined every hour by the passing Lincoln to Doncaster train which rattled and spilled the gin and tonics.

George's target was the roomy public bar. He led the way confidently through the rear door to the room much favoured by personnel from 'the Hall'. Following George closely he could see its attraction. Crowded, it reverberated to a jukebox playing the Beatles' latest hit . The lights were low and the atmosphere thick with layered cigarette smoke.

George threaded his way through the drinkers to reach a space at the bar leaving him to look around recognising faces from the training. They were animated and in the kind of conversation where the background noise forced them to shout to be heard. Silent mouths were singing the 'She loves me yeah, yeah!' refrain of the lyrics. It was soundless and reminded him of the mouths he'd had to watch earlier.

He felt a push on his shoulder.

'Bitter?'

'Yeah, fine.'

Clutching their glasses they moved through the crowd to a space near the door.

'You okay?" George asked.

'Yeah, shouldn't I be?'

'You look a bit fed up.'

He grinned weakly, nice bloke this George. Didn't really know him, it was the typical service life friendship. You meet blokes, complete strangers, hit it off and after five pints you've told 'em your life story and sworn undying friendship. Months later you're off, never to see 'em again.

'Yeah,' he said, 'Thinking about today, all that shit we had to watch. D'ye think it bothers this lot, the civvies I mean?

'Jesus, you are a morbid bugger.' said George, 'You don't realise that they're the lucky ones, most of 'em don't even know or care.

He sipped his drink and nodded, George was right. 'Mind you, you were the one who asked about targets in the lecture, remember, cities and civilians?'

George replied sharply. 'Well why shouldn't I? I asked for everybody. If I'm gonna go, I've told you' I wanna go quick with me family, not survive in a hole with a bunch of fucking strangers.'

It was George's turn to look morose as he slowly sipped his beer. Looking at the usually cheery scouser he blamed himself. The bloke had asked him out for a drink and he'd gone and buggered it up, all because of that shite on the screen. It was now his round and he made his way through the good natured crowd and waited to be served. On the wall at the back of the bar a framed photograph caught his attention. It was a snapshot of its time. A group of smiling young men in flying kit stood huddled beneath the giant wing of an aircraft. As he peered at it a Scots voice said, 'That's me, second left.' It was the barman. A man in his forties with dark greying hair and the lined sallow face of the inveterate smoker.

'Yeah, I recognise you now.' he lied.

'Interested are you?'

'Always have been, heroes the lot of 'em. I couldn't have done it.'

The barman began pulling the required two pints and carried on with the theme.

'That's us, my crew, just before the Dresden trip.'

The photo had been taken prior to take-off, he was the Flight Engineer. They were hit on the way back and he was the sole survivor.

Christ, Dresden!

The barman continued. 'The way it reads today it was a war crime, thousands killed and a cultural treasure destroyed.' The barman was warming to his theme but he knew he'd have to stop him, he'd had enough for one day. Interrupting with

'Well you came out of it okay.' He paid and picked up the beer. Realising his customer was moving away the barman quickly asked, if he was 'up at the Hall?' Receiving a nodded assent he muttered a 'thought so' and turned to another customer. Making his way back to George he handed him his beer. After gulping greedily George wiped his mouth saying, 'You took your time, what did Bob have to say?'

'Bob who?'

'The Landlord, the bloke behind the bar.'

'Oh right, I was interested in his photo, he told me the story."

'Oh yeah, the sole survivor and all that.'

'You're a cynical bugger, he deserves some credit, all his lot do.'

'You're right but I don't know why he's so anti towards us. He likes our money but reckons we're a waste of time. If you listen to him talk he reckons the Yanks run everything and always will and we should leave it all to them and let 'em pay for it.'

This conversation's going nowhere he thought as he glanced around the room and it's all my fucking fault. They were well into the evening and the alcohol had done its work. Lights had been lowered, the music was more insistent and the eyes of the girls were open and shining as their laughter grew louder. He needed to relax. He lit a cigarette and nudged George indicating with his head a table occupied by two girls. There'd been others on that table earlier, he'd been watching. Now it was just the two of them.

'Let's give 'em a try, they've had a few already and we might score.'

At this he began to cough. 'C'mon.' said George, 'Get it up then, better out than in.' His coughing turned to a splutter. George slapped his back. 'I've told you, you ought to pack it in.'

'He's right you know.' said a girl's light voice.

Still spluttering he turned. Through watering eyes he looked at the voice's owner. It was a well built girl in a high necked blouse and short pencil skirt. Christ, he thought, my ship's come home I ought to cough more often. It's better than rubbing a genie's lamp.

'It's the cigarettes, but then you know that don't you?' she said with a smile. He looked at George quizzically then back at the girl. 'You don't recognise me out of uniform do you?'

'C'mon he thought frantically, say something witty and sophisticated you pillock. You don't know her but she knows you but from where? Sensing his confusion she added.

'It's not really a uniform but it might as well be. It's a shop coat remember, when you got off the bus yesterday?'

'Ellie! He almost shouted, it's Ellie from the greengrocer's. She laughed and he joined in more with relief than humour.

'A girl likes to be remembered, it was only yesterday and I'm nearly a nurse so don't think I sell cabbages all day, anyway, who are you?'

Chastened, he introduced himself and rushed into conversation. George, sensing the atmosphere, mouthed a silent 'see you later' and moved away. As they talked he knew his first impressions of her were right. She had an understated good looks that really appealed to him. He'd never gone for the 'in yer face' glamour look although he conceded that service life didn't really support lasting relationships and he winced at the thought of past encounters. A few pints of John Smith's and he'd shag anything. This girl was different. Had she come looking for him he wondered? He knew he'd better not assume that, it would hurt her pride, besides he didn't want to cock things up either.

As if she knew what he was thinking she waved to someone over his shoulder. He felt a sudden pang of jealousy. Christ, don't tell me she's here with another bloke just when I thought I was getting somewhere.

'A friend?' he asked with a forced smile.'

'Three of 'em, old schoolmates. It's a girls' night out.' His relief was almost palpable.

'We meet up when we're home from college, we all go back next week.'

'Oh' he said , 'That's nice.' To himself he thought, there is a God after all!

They chatted, she was a final year nurse at St. Jimmy's in Leeds and only came home some weekends and holidays. That's why she was in her folk's shop helping out.

The room was getting noisier, the Beatles were on again and they were having to shout at each other over the din. He could tell by her occasional glances over his shoulder that she felt she ought to rejoin her friends but he knew he couldn't leave it like this, he had to see her again. As casually as he could be in a shouted conversation he asked her if she'd be here tomorrow?

'Don't think so.' she said. His heart sank. 'Dad doesn't like me coming here really, it's got a bad reputation. He's a Special Constable so I have to be careful."

'Oh I see.' he said with his disappointment showing. Was this the brush off?

She smiled at him. 'Do you like apples?'

'Yes, why do you ask?'

'Pop in the shop tomorrow late afternoon, buy a pound.'

Apples had never sounded so good. Only a pound! He'd buy a sackful and change his name to Bramley!

She turned and picked her way carefully through the drinkers and he watched as he was meant to. He watched the way her waist curved out to her buttocks with every muscle movement emphasized in her tight skirt. He thought back to the lecture with the female scientist. They watch us watching them, always on display. For a woman life was one long presentation.

'Bloody 'ell you've cracked it there no mistake!'

It was George.

'Whaddya mean?' He replied in a voice as ingenuous as he could make it.

'Don't gimme that, I was watching you both, you needed a bucket of cold water throwing over you.'

'Give over, she's alright, a nice kid.'

'Alright! Alright! She's bloody lovely, you jammy bastard!'

He laughed,'Yeah, got to admit that, she's definitely alright, might even see her again.'

The night was coming to an end, they were both intoxicated for different reasons. The clientele was slowly preparing to leave. With beer still in his glass he watched the time honoured ritual of pub leaving time. No one left alone, strangers had paired up or even joined others in loud garrulous groups. Backs were slapped, girls giggled and men burped exaggerated pantomime burps to the delight of all.

Even the sudden tinkle of shattered glass was at home with the amicable bibulous leavetaking. All seemed well until the purposeful figure of the Landlord cleaved its way through the leavetakers to where a small group of people were struggling near the door.

'D'ye see who it is.' shouted George. 'It's that smarmy bastard Instructor, there's a bloke trying to punch his lights out, c'mon this'll be worth watching.'

Two men were struggling with each landing the occasional blow. He recognised the one getting the worst of the encounter. George was right, it was the Instructor. A young woman sobbing and screaming was trying to get between them with the landlord shouting for help in pinning the Instructor's assailant down.

'Bugger .' Said George. 'It's time somebody gave him a good hiding.'

'Who's the other bloke, and the bird?'

'Not sure.' said George. 'He's not with us but I know him from a Mess 'do' at Kenningly. I've a feeling he's a crew chief on the Vulcans'.

The landlord, with help, was holding the Instructor's assailant down allowing him to wriggle free and disappear through the open door into the night leaving the young woman behind still sobbing.

They'd finished their drinks and the excitement had ended much to George's disappointment. His last view of the scene as they left was of the landlord standing and pointing to the door like the old sailor in the 'Boyhood of Raleigh' tableau pointing to the sea. The crew chief and his wife were being banished from the Green Dragon.

As they walked back George agreed that the Instructor's assailant was a 'big bugger' and that he'd catch up with the flash bastard eventually.'

Meandering along the corridor to their respective rooms he bade George goodnight and thanked him.

'What for?' Slurred George.

'Well you did promise me a virgin, remember?'

'Daft sod', Said George and burped loudly.

CHAPTER THREE

That's one good thing about being stationed at a Headquarters he thought, the grub is definitely first class. Headquarters always attract high flyers. The catering officer was no exception. A tall, spare, good humoured man, he possessed a highly developed sense of civilised behaviour which he endeavoured with some success to inculcate upon his staff.

Sitting down in the Mess for breakfast the catering officer's white coated figure smilingly approached him and introduced himself. Exhorting him not to get up he passed him a menu for the coming week to be handed in at his convenience. Looking around him his gaze took in the polished oak tables, silver tableware and crisp white napkins. He'd ordered bacon and egg. He could cope with that in spite of last night's beer. Picking up a newspaper the headlines screamed at him. 'Cuban Missiles Confirmed, US on War Alert.' He read on. 'The US Government has placed its B52 Bomber Force on full nuclear alert. This Alert guarantees that one eighth of the Force will be airborne at any given time. All NATO Allies had been advised to review their own positions. US Forces worldwide were now on DEFCON 3 Alert, a hairsbreadth from full hostilities.'

'Egg and bacon dear, a soft egg like you said.'

The speaker was a middle-aged smiling waitress in starched black and white holding a large breakfast plate.

'Coffee's on its way.' she said, gently placing the plate on the table in front of him.

'I should be careful, it's very hot.' she walked away.

He wanted to scream. Here we go again. 'Don't burn yourself on the hot plate.' What is it with these fucking people, don't they know anything? Here he was surrounded and cosseted by all this middle class comfort, the sodding paper telling him there was a strong possibility of nuclear incineration within the next seven days and a nice granny with a face like a slapped arse was telling him to be careful not to burn his fingers! It was obscene, like when he'd coughed in the lecture. 'Oh dear that's a nasty cough, you ought to be careful. Oh, now where was I? Yes, back to the effects of a nuclear holocaust.'

The egg and bacon didn't taste as good as it looked. He left half and ate toast from the silver rack and mulled over his predicament. He couldn't bank on the Uni holding his place for this year, it was a bastard. All he wanted was a few months, Christ, he'd nearly finished his engagement and now world war three was about to intervene. Not exactly the right climate for their Lordships at the Air Ministry to do him a favour. The newspaper headline was still glaring at him. Who knows he thought grimly, in a week's time there probably won't be an Air Ministry or a Uni.

He still had an hour to kill before starting his first shift so it seemed a good opportunity to check the Orderly Room for any news of his discharge. The office, was one of the old wartime huts above ground. Its utilitarian construction of concrete and asbestos had been offset in a typically English way by the neatly manicured flower beds surrounding it and a crazy paving path leading to its door. He half expected a check trousered Rupert Bear and his Nutwood pals to be in residence when he entered but wasn't disappointed to meet the effete male clerk in charge, with a staff of three giggling female civilians.

Passing his name and number to the Sergeant Clerk, who quickly introduced himself as Ray, he enquired if anything had come through about his discharge? He knew he wasn't supposed to ask but unofficially of course…? He smiled a lot at Ray. He'd really owe him a favour if he could tip him the wink. Ray disappeared into the inner sanctum to look and he was left with the girls. Knowing he was the object of curiosity he ignored them and began to read the file of Station Routine Orders hanging from a notice board.

The most current caught his eye. Headed 'Porton Down CCU', it was an invitation to any public spirited service personnel to spend a fortnight at the Common Cold Research Unit in Wiltshire.

'You're not volunteering for that are you?'

It was Ray back from his search.

'No chance, two weeks with a snotty nose, and taken from your annual leave the greedy sods. They can keep it. Anyway, any luck?'

'Sorry.' said Ray, his eyes soulful. 'Your application's on file, no answer yet but there's a letter caught up with you.' He handed him a well fingered envelope, it was Wigan postmarked, probably from Ernie. I'll read it later he thought stuffing it into a pocket.

'Oh well, no news is good news I suppose.' he smiled winningly at Ray. 'But it'll come through you first won't it?'

'Oh yes, everything does, it has to.' Said Ray importantly. The girls in the background began to giggle. He turned, one look and it was 'eyes down' again.

'Okay, many thanks, be seeing you.'

'You drop by any time,' said Ray. 'You never know I might have something for you.'

He smiled back and thought, 'I'll bet you will.'

The personnel in the Ops Room were unusually quiet. The teleprinters and radios clacked and crackled away incessantly, they were unstoppable. It was the warm buzz of human voices that was missing. At the shift changeover the banter had gone. The usual taking the piss. 'Slept all night then?' 'That's right mate, the Red Menace is all yours for the next eight hours, don't let the bastards wake me, not unless it's summat important.'

No, there was none of that, all humour had been cancelled by the huge red notice on the chinagraph board. 'US Military Alert Posture DEFCON THREE. UK Defence Forces ALERT STATE RED.

It was as if a darkness had enveloped him. He looked at the others, about thirty of them calmly calculating, listening, poring over charts and maps or just sat with faces blank and expressionless. That's what we are now, he thought, functionaries, automatons. Welcome to our new family, we lose our real ones and we create a new one from this lot. This was his first shift in the Ops Room where to his surprise he found his office to be a glass surrounded space. The Room itself was the newest structure at the Headquarters. Almost a large barn, open and spacious and built of brick with wide windows set in each of the four walls. This building wasn't meant to survive, it was purely functional containing as it did one wall covered with a map of Europe and European Russia. The notations on the map indicating airfields and missile sites told their own story in the confrontation between East and West. All functions in the Room such as Communications, Radar, Logistics had their own sectioned off working area, all in full view of the Senior Operations Officer with his staff placed high on the raised platform overlooking every activity. He was 'Codes and Ciphers.' His role was to accept from Bomber Command HQ at High Wycombe all coded high priority signals and put them into 'plain language' to be passed on to the operations officers.

The rattling, clattering and squawking continued. The giant clocks showing times in different zones clicked monotonously and inexorably on. He lit a cigarette and felt for the unopened letter in his pocket. He didn't recognise the handwriting but the postmark was Wigan which was Ernie's neck of the woods.

As he read his stomach felt empty, his face flushed and his eyes filled. Fuck it! It can't be right. He read on. It was from Amy, Ernie's wife, it was a week old. Ernie's condition had worsened and was now terminal necessitating a move to a hospice. There was a 'phone number and an address. 'I know he'd like to see you, try and make it soon' she'd written. The finality of her request with all its implications overwhelmed him. Deliberately dropping his cigarette under his desk he bent down to retrieve it brushing the tears away, ashamed and angry at his weakness.

Sat upright again he pondered on the rapid deterioration in Ernie's health. He'd been okay in Maralinga at the nuclear tests. He was as fit as a fiddle, he'd proved that. Mind you if a fucking great dingo was after a piece of my arse, he thought, I'd run like hell.

He laughed to himself recalling the incident. It made him feel better. That's what good times were for he supposed, pity Amy and her kid couldn't share it with him.

Above the activity the internal tannoy was being tested. 'One, two, three, four, five.' An expensive sounding metallic voice intoned. 'Listen in gentlemen listen in.'

It was the 'gentlemen' bit again. 'Gentlemen' in his experience conveyed bad news. It was a 'poisoned chalice' usually meaning there'd be shit coming in their direction. The voice exhorted them to continue with their duties but to be alert and ready for further instructions. He listened but like everyone else in the room he wanted to know where the voice came from. Funny, he thought, how we all automatically look up, like being at an air display. The tannoy speakers were located in every upper corner of the room. The voice was elaborating on the seriousness of the international situation and that to test readiness, sometime during the day, the four minute warning would be implemented. The nuclear armed Vulcan bombers at Kenningly and the other four airfields under Granby's control would all go 'operational' which meant a mass take-off over the local area. Personnel instructions were to then to disappear down into the bunker but to remain on the premises until the test was over.

The voice's final heartwarming piece of information was that 'the enemy would begin its attack on the UK by detonating a nuclear warhead high over the North Sea. The resultant energy burst would destroy all communications systems. The main attack would follow within minutes'. Welcome to a wasteland.

The test came when he was on the 'phone. When the klaxons screeched their warning there was no rush. He patted his pockets, yeah, fags and lighter all there. Crossing the room he joined the orderly queue down the narrow stairs to the bunker. The klaxons had stopped, being superseded by a dull all enveloping rumble.

'Christ!' Shouted a voice, 'come up here, take a look at this.'

With others he left his place in the queue and stared upward through the window into the sharp, clear October sky. The rumble was growing even greater as he placed his hands over his ears. It reminded him of the tests in Maralinga. They'd all stood like this then, amazed at the skeletal sight of their own bones. A lone white bomber climbing high was being joined by others, he counted them and stopped at eight, as with numbers swelling the aircraft rose higher and higher with engines labouring on full power. With hands still over his ears he watched with a sick fascination and felt the whole world vibrate around him as the aircraft headed east. They were still cheering when the rumbling had subsided and he'd descended into the refined air of the bunker.

The afternoon was his until six o'clock when he was back on watch. It was time to buy those apples. Still in uniform and with a cigarette cupped out of sight in his hand he strode cheerfully along toward the main street. An old couple were walking towards him. She was limping and using a stick, the old man stared in his direction as they drew closer and smiled broadly as their paths were about to cross. He smiled and nodded back. What had the old man seen? He didn't know him from Adam. Did his youth and vitality remind the old man of himself years ago? Had he recognised the age old signs of a young serviceman's eager anticipation in meeting a girl? As they passed he looked back at them. With his pace adjusted to accommodate the unsteady walk of his partner the old man's back seemed to straighten as he placed a supporting arm around the woman.

It was the one day of the week when the main street was busy and difficult to cross. Its new found solitude being disrupted by the traditional market day with stalls and increased local traffic. At the traffic lights he joined a small crocodile of schoolchildren with a teacher. Waiting for the lights to change the kids were eyeing him up curiously in his blue uniform.

'Hey mister, were you in them planes this morning? They didn't half make a noise.' said one.

'Yeah'. From another, 'My dad says they're full o' bombs as well, is that right mister?'

'Don't be daft ,' said another 'They only have bombs when there's a war on, that's right innit mister?'

The young teacher raised her eyebrows and smiled indulgently at him as the red light halted the flow of traffic allowing them to cross. His interrogators refused to give up as they skipped and ran alongside him.

'There isn't a war is there mister, my dad says there isn't.'

He looked down at the concerned freckled face. 'No, 'course not, we're only practising.'

He looked again at the fresh smooth innocence, other images imposed themselves, noiseless in black and white, he paused and said again, 'course not.'

Peering through the shop window he could see Ellie serving. With her hair pinned back and wearing her shop coat it was a complete contrast to her appearance in the pub. When the shop emptied he entered. 'I haven't forgotten my apples.' She smiled, 'I do like you in your uniform, you look really smart.' He grinned. 'I like you in yours.'

'Work's work, you should see me in my nurse's outfit!'

'Can't wait.' he said , leering and rolling his eyes.

She reddened and he knew he'd gone too far and embarrassed her. He thought she'd said it suggestively, had she? He didn't know. She quickly changed the subject.

'That noise this morning it was tremendous, the whole town rattled, what were they doing? I've never seen so many of 'em before.'

He told her about the four minute warning and how all the aircraft had to be ready. Didn't she know how things were?'

'I don't really take much notice.' she said, carefully selecting four apples and polishing them. 'I don't think anybody does.' She thought the four minute warning was just a military thing. There was nothing ordinary people could do anyway, there were no shelters, especially in Granby although they did give her dad a siren because he was the local Special Constable. Civil defence sounded alright in theory, she knew about that from her nursing training. But

DENIS PRICE

what was the point? These new atom bombs would destroy everything.

She put the apples in a bag. 'There you are sir, that'll be ninepence halfpenny please.' She assumed a brisk business like tone. He laughed and examined his change. 'It's either sevenpence or a pound note.'

'Oh go on then, pay up next time.'

A door banged at the back of the shop and a woman in her forties entered wearing a shop coat similar to Ellie's. She looked questioningly at him, his uniform, and the bag of apples.

'Er, yes that's ninepence halfpenny.' Ellie said.

He gave her a pound note and apologised for having no change. The woman looked from one to the other knowingly.

'Who's this then?'

Ellie introduced him to her mother. 'This is Dan.'

'You're up at the Hall ?' It was almost an accusation.

He explained he was new and didn't know how long he'd be there. Keep it brief but polite he thought. It was obvious that mum wasn't keen on fly by nights from the Hall, her daughter was meant for better things. He'd had these interrogations before, mums were worse than dads. In an attempt to reassure he found himself telling her about taking up a university place, this year if the service would let him out. He sensed a thaw at this revelation and the atmosphere relaxed. Mum moved further down the shop to check the stock.

Conversation was difficult with Ellie's mother within hearing, even an arrangement to meet again, when and where? Suddenly it was solved. 'We're out of King Edwards.' She called out. 'Perhaps your friend 'll give you a hand.'

Ellie looked across at him and smiled. 'C'mon, they're in the store, I'll show you the siren as well if you like?'

The family lived above and at the back of the shop. In the rear yard was a flat roofed, concrete fruit and vegetable store. Following her into the yard he was entranced watching her pinned back hair bob up and down in time with the fluid movement of her hips, visible under her thin shop coat. He felt his body harden as they entered the store. She flicked the light switch with no response. 'Damn!' She said. 'Stay close to me or you'll trip over something, the potatoes are further back.' He sensed the signals and deliberately pressed his hardness against her body grinding himself against her. She turned and kissed him as his hands reached for her breasts. She held his wrists. 'No not here, not now, I'm sorry, we can't.' Anger and frustration made him push her away. 'I'm sorry, but it wouldn't be right' She said, 'try and understand, there'll be another time, I need time, please understand.'

He knew she was right but would there be another time and another place? If only he could share her optimism. She found the sack and he carried it to the door. 'Leave it there for now and I'll show you the siren.'

With his body still hard and aching he followed her to a ladder propped up against the wall of the store.

'You first.' She said self consciously smoothing down her shop coat. At the top he reached down and held her hand as she climbed the ladder. Desire welled up again as she gripped his hand tightly and he eased her on to the roof. He gently pulled her toward him, she kissed him lightly.' The whole world can see us up here you know, '

'So what?'

'C'mon,' She said briskly, this is dad's siren.' She pointed to a large tarpaulin covered box and began to remove the cover. Underneath was a cylindrical drum with a cranking handle bracketed on its underside.

'This is it?' he said, unconvinced.

'Yeah, it's dad's job to operate it when that warning you mentioned is given.'

'Isn't there a powered one somewhere? I saw a civil defence film the other day and they were powered.'

'I don't know about that.' She said. 'There's an electric one at the police station but dad says it's not very reliable. This is a back up. It's definitely manual. He tests it when he feels like it.'

He cast his mind back to the film with its utopian depiction of civil defence, Christ, these people had the right idea, why worry? There's no point to any of it, they're all goners anyway.

She was first down the ladder. Showing off he jumped down landing almost next to her. 'That was silly, you could have broken something.' He began to cough, he thought it was probably the exertion. His coughing persisted and he began to retch with his face reddening. Concerned, she told him to try and breathe deeply. He leaned back on the ladder for support. She was looking at him concerned, speaking firmly she told him, 'It's the smoking, you really should cut it down.' It was a wonderful feeling to be admonished by her, he was elated that she cared.

'C'mon.'she said. 'Mum'll want her spuds.'

CHAPTER FOUR

St. Margaret's it said on the board, St. Margaret's Catholic Hospice. He wondered, did you have to be a Catholic to die here? I suppose Catholics think you have to be. It was a stupid conjecture brought about by irrational fear. He felt too young, too inexperienced to be visiting this place of death. This was a place steeped in experience and memory, both fellow travellers of age. Ernie was young, life loving and laughing. He was a mate who'd lend you his last quid and outrun the biggest, angriest, fucking dingo in the world. Sat in his hired car in the visitor's car park his eyes filled. He was angry again, angry with himself and his emotions. Driving across the windswept Pennines he'd told himself 'Stay strong and be positive. Think good things, blot it out. Think Ellie, think university, blot it all out.' But that's being disloyal to Ernie, you can't blot out flesh and blood like you can a screen of black and white images.

He felt the irritation start in his chest which started him coughing, his mind began to race back to the images and then to Ernie, flesh and blood Ernie. It was time.

Ernie was in a room of four. Tense and apprehensive

with a forced smile, he gazed at the occupant of each bed as they lay propped up against pillows with sallow almost oriental faces in sharp contrast with the brilliant white bed linen. Mouths were open and round as they greedily sucked in life giving oxygen through transparent masks. Past images returned to him. An arm was raised weakly from a corner bed. The frail emaciated figure smiled broadly with the head remaining still on the pile of pillows as he rushed over to the bedside.

'You bugger!' said Ernie in a hoarse voice. ' What took you so long?'

'Ern, you malingering sod, what the hell are you doing in here?'

He moved forward and gently hugged the frail figure using the opportunity to hide his tears. It was a test, after the initial shock he knew he'd come out of it. Amy had prepared him for Ernie's condition in her letter but it was still hard to reconcile the fit bloke of a year ago with the childlike husk lying in front of him. He chose to sit on the bed rather than on a chair. They talked about everything with Ernie deflecting the conversation away from his illness, asking him about his life and his hopes for the future, each recognising the finality of their words. He told him about meeting Ellie and university, how he felt things were starting to gell. They talked old times, Maralinga and the awesome witnessing of the nuclear tests, the dingo that wouldn't die then of course they got round to Amy and young Matt. They were coming tomorrow. It always gave Ernie a lift although he didn't like the boy seeing him there. He fell silent, then spoke again.

'Keep an eye on 'em for me won't you, he's a clever lad he'll go places I know he will,'

Struggling to keep his voice firm and reassuring he replied.'C'mon Ern you miserable bugger, you'll still be around to take care of 'em.'

The huge brown eyes set in the sallow emaciated face locked on to him, holding him in their thrall.

'We both know better than that, don't we?'

Releasing him from his hypnotic grip Ernie peered over his shoulder, smiling.

'You'll have to go now, it's happy hour.'

'Happy hour?'

'Yeah, we all love happy hour, time for our joy juice. Beats six cans o' Tiger any day.'

'What is it?'

'Diamorphine, heroin to the likes of you and me. The dreams I've had, you wouldn't believe it!' You see the big bloke, the staff nurse?'

'Yeah.'

'That's Harry, guess how he gives it to us, go on?'

'In a drip, mebbe a jab in your arm?'

'Wrong, he sticks it up my arse!'

'You're kiddin'!'

'No, it's a French method of pain relief, so he tells me. They put the drug in a big capsule and Harry sticks it up me fundament.'

'You're not havin' me on are you?'

'Well Harry swears it's a capsule he's stickin' in."

The both paused for a second and then chanting in

unison, almost shouted, 'So was he in the Navy or did he go to public school?' Then they laughed.

It was a well rehearsed routine from way back, adolescent he knew, but always good for a laugh.

The staff nurse approached with his trolley full of dreams and he knew it was time to go. Leaning forward he lightly hugged the shrunken figure. 'I'd better be off, see you next week Ern,' It was the eyes again, his were full and Ernie's were huge and hypnotic.

'Yeah 'course you will, ring Amy won't you?'

He stepped away from the bed as the curtains closed silently around it.

He remembered little of the drive back. The swooping dipping Pennine roads which normally exhilarated him, he left to the joy of others as they roared past him celebrating this natural rollercoaster. Dropping down to the eastern flatlands he pulled in at a roadside garage for fuel. It was a lonely night for travellers, he was the only customer on the premises. Inside at the cash desk a tired looking television set surrounded by Liquorice Allsorts and Coca Cola had a newsreader announcing that nuclear submarines were moving into the Caribbean off Cuba. High overhead he could hear the giant unseen rumble of an aircraft. Waiting for his change he looked nervously skyward into the darkness.

'One of ours is it?' Said the middle-aged male attendant sarcastically, handing him his change.

'I hope so.'

'You've been watching too much of this crap.' Said the attendant, stabbing at the television button, exchanging news of the world's inexorable advance toward nuclear holocaust for the anodyne 'Opportunity Knocks!'

'Yeah, I think you're right,' he said as he closed the door behind him.

Arriving back at Granby he checked in at the guardroom and went to his room. The accommodation block was quiet, even the spider had disappeared although the web had gained another dried out husk. It had been a long draining day, he needed company and he was hungry. It was too late to visit Ellie and after knocking on George's door with no response he guessed he'd be in the pub. He knew he'd have to eat first and with the Mess closed the only place in town was the Chippy, a favourite with late night carousers. The shop was off the main street, half way up a narrow lane of terraced houses whose occupants lives must have been made unbearable by the late night antics of drunken customers.

Inside the Chippy it was warm and inviting and he had the place to himself. Leaning forward on the shining stainless steel counter his body luxuriated in the warmth exuding from the open fryer.

'Oppen or tekkout?'

'Open.' He answered the terse question with similar brevity. He was a man of few words the Chippy owner, words didn't sell chips. With typical scouse humour George had remarked that getting speech out of him was ' like getting shit from a rocking horse!' After generously applying salt and vinegar he left the brightness of the shop, stepping out into the gloom of the narrow lane with his attention focused on his food.

As he recalled later, it all happened in a second. A

blinding pain on the side of his head, then his face lying on the cold footpath and then a more sharp incisive pain from a blow to his ribs, probably from a boot. A rushing sound in his ears and distant shouting was all he could recall until he woke up sat in a chair in the back room of the Chippy.

The Chippy man had heard a noise, found him and brought him back to the shop. Sat in the chair he'd been given a poultice which he was holding over his right eye with his left one taking in the state he was in. No wonder he was overwhelmed with the smell of fish and chips, he was covered in 'em! He'd obviously fallen on the whole parcel. Question was , who the fuck had done it and why? He'd hardly been at Granby long enough to piss anybody off, unless like George had said, it was the local lads evening up the score!

There was plenty of time for him to ponder on these matters on the journey to Doncaster Infirmary. During treatment the police questioned him but what could he tell 'em? The friendly casualty doctor told him he'd got off lightly. They'd X-Rayed him which showed a couple of cracked ribs which he'd had strapped up and he also had a shiner. No drink involved either, the doctor said it made a change. He was offered a bed or a lift back, he took the latter. After visiting Ernie he couldn't stay in a hospital.

CHAPTER FIVE

He decided to report for duty although he knew he could probably have the day off if he asked. As he limped into the Mess he was conscious of the sidelong glances. Every footstep pierced his chest. Wheezing, he sat down and reached out to the silver toast rack. A hand reached over him. 'There, there, dear,' said the rosy cheeked waitress maternally. 'You have been in the wars, let me do it.' He turned painfully to thank her, exposing the full extent of his black eye. She winced. 'Ooh! Whoever did that?'

He answered.' I wish I knew, I wish I knew.'

She withdrew, clucking as she went.

Morosely he sat alone, every bite made his face throb and his teeth ache. The newspapers were in but he wasn't interested. The visit on Ernie and the beating had taken its toll. In a nutshell, he'd fucking well had enough! One wrong word from anybody today and they'd cop the lot, he didn't care who the fucking hell it was, that's all it had to be, one wrong word.

'Marmalade?' Said a fey voice from behind him. He tensed. 'Can I have the marmalade?' The voice's owner came into view, it was Ray the chief clerk. Taking the marmalade Ray registered horror at the sight of his eye. Before he could comment he told him. 'Just don't ask, don't ask!' Regretting his tone and in an attempt to retrieve the situation he told him he felt rough and would he like to join him knowing that marmalade wouldn't be the only topic of conversation.

Sitting down at the table and fastidiously re-arranging the cutlery Ray told him his news.

'Something's come through about your application, be ready for an interview later this morning, can't say any more.' His tone was conspiratorial.

'Is that it?

'I can't open the Adjutant's mail,' Said Ray, hurt.'

'I'm sorry Ray, 'course you can't,' He said. 'I'm just being a pillock.'

Back at work he ignored the curious glances and accepted the handover from the shift going off duty. It was the usual stuff but with more of an edge to it, like he'd noticed earlier, the fun had gone. He checked the logs, nothing untoward there. The frequencies and codes used to contact the bombers were changed on a daily basis, it was his job to verify the changes. Yeah, he thought, we're all ready and equipped to blow each other to fucking smithereens. Mebbe we should all watch 'Opportunity Knocks' instead, the world might be a better place. He wondered if the Russians had a version of it?

He was on his third cigarette when the call came, a replacement took over. Report to the Adjutant's office the note said, nothing else, no indication of the reason or topic to be discussed, he didn't like the sound of it at all, it just wasn't positive. The office was in the grounds of the Hall. His heavy service shoes crunched on the horse chestnuts hidden among the leaves as he limped up the path. Adjusting his hat he entered to be met by the Adjutant's clerk. He looked at the man's face for an encouraging sign, it was expressionless. Almost swallowing his pride and asking outright, his intention was cut short by a curt 'Follow me.' The clerk took him to the door , knocked and left . A voice called out 'Come in!'

He entered, saluted smartly and winced at the effort. The Adjutant sat in a comfortable chair in front of a cluttered desk. He was a jolly balding man, his face bristling with an aggressive moustache. His office walls were decorated with the usual wartime photographs and some of a woman with children, obviously his family. Staring intently at his visitor, he commented. 'Good God man, that is a black eye. How on earth did you manage that?" Not waiting for an answer he chuckled. 'At ease, you can sit there if you like.' He pointed to the room's other chair.

They sat looking at each other for seconds, he could see his personal file open on the desk. The Adjutant didn't mess about, he'd like to tell him otherwise but his application had been turned down. It happened to all of us at some time or other he commented, the platitudes poured out, exigencies of the service, political situation uncertain. He wasn't listening any more, his eye throbbed and his ribs ached and his mind raced. The Adjutant paused to watch his reaction.

'Is there anything else Sergeant?

'No sir, thank you.' He got up and saluted.

Walking away with anger enveloping him he muttered

'Thank you sir, thank you for fuck all!' The clerk walked to the door with him. 'Sorry mate, you never know with these applications, try again in six months, I would.' He thanked him and limped back to the Ops Room.

That night he knew he had to go for a drink, it'd been a shit day all round. George had already left for the pub and he'd arranged to meet him there. It was early so they had the place almost to themselves. Sitting in silence they sipped their beer in the measured way that solitary drinkers do. Not driven by the needs of conversation to drink with enthusiasm, it was just an exercise to dull the senses. He knew that in this situation he could drink almost forever before the alcohol found him. George, being aware of his disappointment broke the silence.

'D'ye remember that business the other night? When flash bastard nearly got his come-uppance.'

'So?'

'Well that big bloke from Kenningly was in here last night.'

'Yeah.'

'Yeah, he was looking for him and his wife, pissed out of his mind he was. Bob buggered him off. Wouldn't like to meet up with him on a dark night, 'specially the mood he was in.'

Listening to George he lit another cigarette. His numbed thought processes were slipping into gear. 'What time was this?'

'Just before closing, why, you didn't bump into him did you?'

He didn't answer but some things were becoming clearer, or were they? He wasn't sure.

He began to cough, the sharp pain in his ribs stabbed repeatedly in time with his spasms. Fucking great, he thought, Ellie said she'd try and drop in tonight, he couldn't go 'round her place looking like this , her dad would go apeshit!

Good old George was just telling him not to worry in that friendly avuncular way that seemed to be his trademark when Bob the Landlord approached their table. ' Sorry lads, drink up, you're wanted back at the Hall, just had 'em on the 'phone.'

'You're kiddin!'

'Definitely not, d'ye think I wanna lose customers?'

He looked around, Bob was now talking to several others who were grudgingly finishing their drinks.

'S'pose we'd better make a move.' said George. 'Bob's too fuckin' greedy to be kiddin'.'

In desultory two's and three's they all made their way back to the Hall, he guessed 'something was up', Was it gonna be an even shittier end to an already shit day? Shielding his eyes from the neon glare of the Ops Room he realised as he looked around that he was only one of many. All three shifts of personnel were in attendance, crammed into whatever chair or space they could find and wondering what was going on?

The speculation was dispelled as a voice called the room smartly to attention and an Air Vice Marshal entered.

Christ almighty, he thought, where did he spring from, Madam Tussauds? He'd never seen one o' these before. The man was tall and impressive, wearing his formal uniform with a chest full of wings, medals and decorations. An acolyte passed him a chair which to everyone's surprise he stood upon rather than sat. 'Gentlemen.' He called out, addressing the room from his commanding height. Yeah, he thought as he watched the man's performance, yeah, it's that word again. Shit is definitely heading our way. 'Gentlemen, I have to advise you that the military and political situation between the Soviets and ourselves has deteriorated.' He continued. 'The situation is now that Soviet Missile Batteries on the island of Cuba have shot down a USAF U2 Reconnaisance aircraft killing the pilot and Soviet missile carrying vessels are approaching the 'quarantine' or blockade line imposed by President Kennedy. I must tell you that if these vessels do not stop or turn away in the next few hours, United States Naval Units will carry out their orders. The ensuing military action will then involve us all. Remember gentlemen the next few hours will be crucial to the fate of the Free World. Those of you who are not on duty may now retire to your quarters and God speed to you all.'

The Officer's chair scraped the floor as he climbed down. It was the only sound other than that of the equipment. People silently left the room. George looked fierce and determined in a way he hadn't seen before. 'I'm off back home,' he said adamantly. 'If it's that bad that's where we all belong, with our folks.'

It was his turn to give reassurance but he couldn't, there wasn't any to give. Instead he told him 'Don't be a prat, you'll never get off the Camp, not now, you might as well stay.'

He sat at his position busying himself with the decoding of fuel capacities, radio frequencies and meteorological forecasts knowing that out on the tarmac only a few miles away the whole nuclear bomber force was waiting to take off. Each aircraft carrying its own little parcels of instant sunshine. His thoughts drifted to Ellie, her parents, the shop, the main street, the Green Dragon. Would it be a wasteland by morning, would the siren be unused? The old couple and the schoolkids what of them?' 'My dad says there isn't a war, is there mister?' Then there was Bob, the destroyer of Dresden, would he survive this night as he did the night over Germany? All imponderables to him and yet they were all secure, safe and secure in their own ignorance. They were the lucky ones.

The hours passed and the noise subsided. The clocks ticked their hammer blows eating away at the time as coffee was passed around. 'No sugar for me thanks,' he said. 'I'm trying to give it up.'

Before dawn the Air Vice Marshal decided to speak again, this time over the tannoy. It was a 'why we are here and why we are doing this' kind of speech. Sat at his far position he deliberately put earphones on to blot it out. In spite of this he could hear more references to 'the Free World' and Red Expansionism' and it seemed as always that 'God was with us.' It wasn't exactly Larry Olivier doing St. Crispin's Day, but fair do's he thought, Larry wasn't about to incinerate twenty million people. He looked across at George, the lucky sod was asleep.

It was about seven o'clock when the red 'phone began its strident ringing. Years later when people said they remembered where and what they were doing when Kennedy was assassinated he would remember that room and that time. The silent sea of grey night strained faces all turning to the man picking up the 'phone. Do we live or do we die?

Would he see Ellie again with her smiling brown eyes? The shop with it's gleaming apples. Would the old folks draw next week's pension and was the kid's dad right about war? Bob's grandkids might never learn of how he survived Dresden. He watched the Air Vice Marshal's mouth tighten, every line of sweat and stubble on his face was studied by forty pairs of eyes. Then slowly his lips drew back to reveal strong white teeth, he smiled! Watching from afar he knew then that Good had triumphed over Evil. God was with us after all, the missiles were going home and so was he. An involuntary cheer went up. A now awake George hugged his cracked ribs until he cried out with the pain. There was laughter and backslapping, all the tension disappeared. He looked around and thought, I'm in the winner's enclosure at Ascot, England have won the World Cup and Susannah York wants to have her wicked way with me, oh, and the bastards are going to release me. But he knew the reality. The Air Marshal would get another medal, his underlings would be promoted, and him? Well he'd miss the early breakfast.

George was buoyant as they emerged into the crisp autumn air. 'C'mon.' He said, 'Bugger the Mess, I'll stand us a fry-up at the caff'. The offer was a good one, the Angel Café was on the main street almost opposite Ellie's shop, he might catch her opening up for the day. With new found energy George stepped out briskly in the crisp cold air. 'C'mon you poor old bugger, get a move on,' he shouted. Gulping in the air he couldn't match George's pace, he winced at each intake of breath and his ribs ached. Slowing down to a walking pace he looked around the street and wondered at the events of the night. Everything was in focus, sharper and better defined.

People with red morning faces, animated and laughing. A car horn blared impatiently, a bell rang on a schoolboy's bike. Ellie's mother was laying out fruit in the shop window. Raising himself on his toes he could even see the top of the sinister siren thankfully unused on the roof of the store. He stood staring and drank it all in. 'You lucky, lucky buggers, you just don't know.'

After breakfast at the Angel they re-entered the Camp striding through the leaf strewn grounds only stopping occasionally to allow George to aim horse chestnuts at scurrying squirrels.

'They're a bit of a novelty to me, squirrels, we don't see many in Liverpool.'

'You've probably eaten 'em all.'

The path led them past the Orderly Room. 'Hey', said George, 'somebody's waving at us, at the window, see?' Christ he thought, it's not Ray again, he wasn't really in the mood for his small talk. The clerk was at the door now waving excitedly. George grinned and said with an exaggerated leer 'I think I'll leave you to it,' and walked off. Limping cautiously along the leaf strewn crazy paving toward the animated Ray, he just managed a grin before the clerk blurted out a message, 'Report to the Sick Quarters as soon as possible, the doctor wants an urgent word, probably lost your records when you moved here.'

The doctor was waiting for him' 'Ah! Sergeant, glad I caught you.' he said engagingly. 'Do sit down there's something I must discuss with you, it's rather urgent.' Christ he thought, what's this all about? His mind returned to the events of the other night. It wasn't nice but it was only a bit of a kicking.

'I've had your X-Ray results forwarded to me and in view of what they reveal I'm recommending that you see a specialist in the next few days for further investigation.'

He sat, stunned. No, he wouldn't like a glass of water or a cup of tea.

'Do you smoke?' Asked the doctor.

He told him about twenty a day, more on the night shift. The Doctor explained, 'You've been very lucky but you're not out of the wood yet. The X-Ray on your ribs has revealed a possible abnormality on the right lung, we'll have to carry out further investigation of course.' He felt sick. The doctor continued, 'Are you sure you wouldn't like a glass of water?'

'He answered. 'I'd rather have a smoke.'

The Doctor looked at him hard. 'If you must.' He continued. 'I've seen your record, you were at Maralinga for the Tests.'

'Yeah, all of 'em, so what's that got to do with it?'

'Nothing I shouldn't think, just curious.'

'This investigation you mention, where does it leave me?'

Oh! There'll be a Medical Board of course, we'll have to discharge you, we haven't the facilities. You'll be treated by your local National Health Body, you're from Hull I believe?'

'You mean I'll be discharged?'

'On the Board's recommendations within days I should think, on medical grounds. We'll make the arrangements and pass your records…'

He began to laugh uncontrollably, the laugh became a

retching cough. With streaming eyes distorting his vision he stood up, leaning forward to seek support from the doctor's desk. After handing him a tissue the Doctor carefully picked up his files and left, quietly closing the door behind him.

Lightning Source UK Ltd.
Milton Keynes UK
24 September 2010
160315UK00001B/5/P